To M, H, and R for your love and support —JB

All rights reserved. Published in the United States by Doubleday,
an imprint of Random House Children's Books, a division of Penguin Random House LLC, New York.
Originally published in Australia by Little Hare Books, an imprint of Hardie Grant, in 2016.

Doubleday and the colophon are registered trademarks of Penguin Random House LLC.

Visit us on the Web! randomhousekids.com

Educators and librarians, for a variety of teaching tools,
visit us at RHTeachersLibrarians.com

Library of Congress Cataloging-in-Publication Data
Names: Bentley, Jonathan, author, illustrator.
Title: Where is bear? / by Jonathan Bentley.
Description: New York : Doubleday, [2017] | Summary: "A little boy and his
best friend—an actual bear—go on a search for a teddy bear before
bedtime." —Provided by publisher. | "Originally published in Australia by
Little Hare Books, an imprint of Hardie Grant, in 2016."
Identifiers: LCCN 2016013076 | ISBN 978-0-399-55593-0 (hc) — ISBN 978-0-399-55651-7 (ebook)
Subjects: | CYAC: Teddy bears—Fiction. | Bears—Fiction. | Toys—Fiction. |
Bedtime—Fiction.
Classification: LCC PZ7.1.B4545 Wh 2017 | DDC [E]—dc23

MANUFACTURED IN CHINA

10 9 8 7 6 5 4 3 2 1

First American Edition

The illustrations in this book were created using pencil and watercolors.

Where is Bear?

Jonathan Bentley

Doubleday Books for Young Readers

Where is Bear?

Where could Bear be?

Is Bear in the drawer?

Is Bear on the shelf?

Where is Bear?

I saw him somewhere.
But where?

In the bathroom?

Downstairs?

Is Bear on the table?

Is Bear under the sofa?

Where is Bear?

Where could Bear be?

On the swing?

In the car?

I just don't know.
I'm getting tired.

I want to sleep. . . .

Where is Bear?

Have you seen Bear?

What? Where?

Where is Bear?

Oh, there is Bear!

I found him, Bear!

Here is *your* bear.

Good night, Bear.
Good night, Bear.